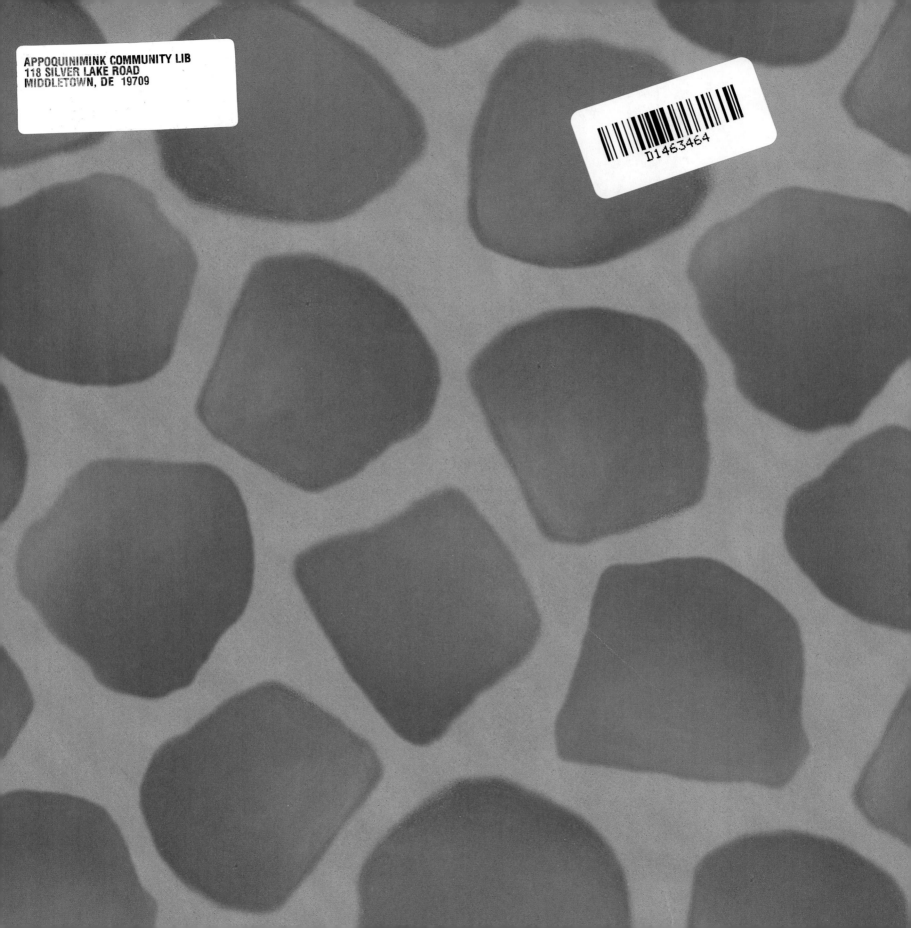

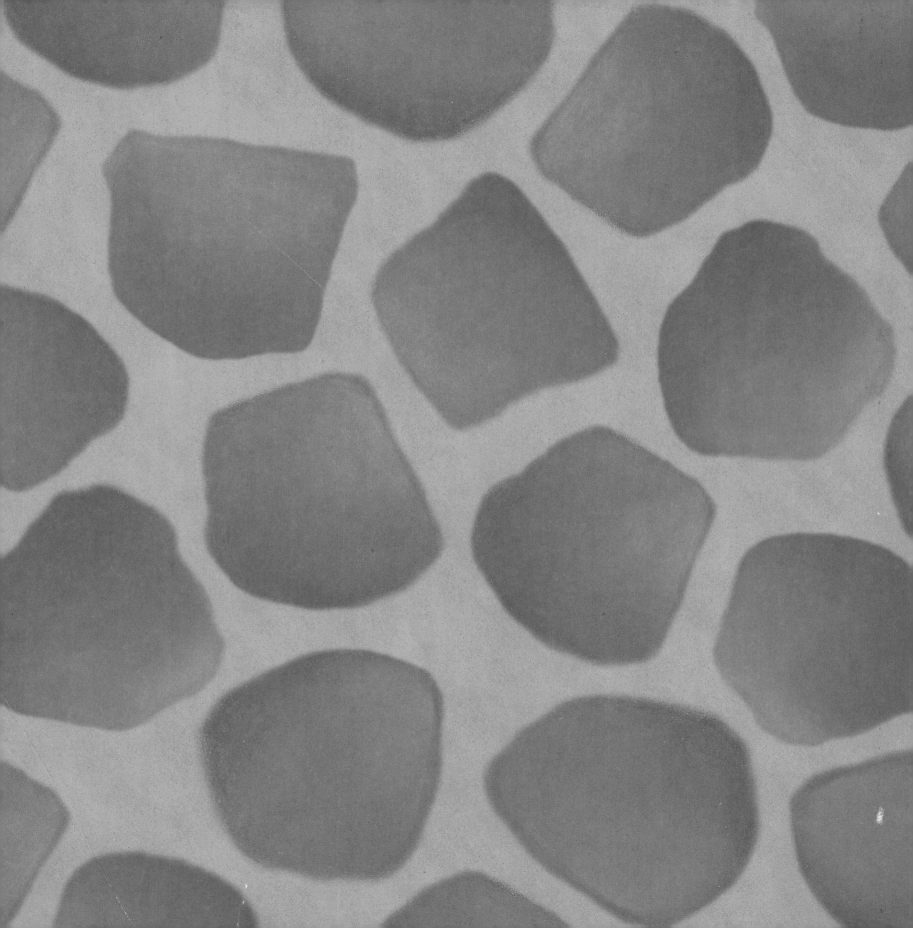

Gilda and Friends

Lucky

An orphan leopard
cub who has the
worst luck

Pepin

A persistent
penguin who loves
his family

Marvin

A silly little
marmoset who is
afraid of heights

Ernest

A young elephant who is
very afraid of mice

Gilda

A friendly giraffe who
loves melons and parties

Zander

A caring,
wise zebra who looks
out for his friends

Leonardo

An adventurous little
lion cub who likes to
go exploring

Papaya

A lovable panda who
eats a lot of bamboo

Turnip

A spirited young
turtle who loves an
adventure

*We hope you enjoy the many adventures of Gilda and Friends. Our goal was to maintain the spirit of the
original French-language story while adapting it to the Picture Window Books' format. Thank you to the
original publisher, author, and illustrator for allowing Picture Window Books to make this series available
to a new audience.*

Editor: Jacqueline A. Wolfe
Page Production: Tracy Kaehler
Creative Director: Keith Griffin
Editorial Director: Carol Jones
Managing Editor: Catherine Neitge

First American edition published in 2006 by
Picture Window Books
5115 Excelsior Boulevard
Suite 232
Minneapolis, MN 55416
877-845-8392
www.picturewindowbooks.com

First published in Canada in 2000 by
Les éditions Héritage inc.
300 Arran Street
Saint Lambert, Quebec
Canada J4R 1K5

Printed in the United States of America.

Library of Congress Cataloging-in-Publication Data
Papineau, Lucie.
Gilda the giraffe and Pepin the penguin / by Lucie Papineau ; illustrated by Marisol Sarrazin.
p. cm. "Gilda the giraffe."
Summary: Becoming lost while on a fishing trip, Pepin the penguin must rely on his new friends in a strange
land to help him find the way home to his family.
ISBN 1-4048-1296-2 (hardcover)
[1. Penguins—Fiction. 2. Animals—Fiction.] I. Sarrazin, Marisol, 1965—ill. II. Title.
PZ7.P2115Gile 2005
[E]—dc22
2005011347

Gilda the Giraffe
and
Pepin the Penguin

by Lucie Papineau
illustrated by Marisol Sarrazin
story adapted by Michael Dahl

PICTURE WINDOW BOOKS
Minneapolis, Minnesota

Far, far away, in a land that is perfectly cold and perfectly white, lives Pepin the penguin. Pepin lives with his pretty wife Penelope and his plump chicks Pistachio and Peanut.

One fine morning, Pepin went fishing by the icy shore. The weather was warm and pleasant. The water was still, without a breath of wind.

While Pepin fished, he stared at the calm waves. He stared at his pole. He did not notice that the ice he was sitting on was melting. Soon, he was floating on a small iceberg far, far out to sea.

The hot sun melted the small iceberg until Pepin was perched on nothing more than a big ice cube.

Pepin looked around and found himself near a strange shore. Many new and unusual animals were looking at him.

"Where am I?" asked Pepin.

"You are in the jungle," replied Gilda the giraffe.

"This place is not cold or white," said Pepin. "I am very far from home. My family must be worried about me."

"We will help you find your way back," offered Gilda.

Her friend Camelot the camel nodded. "With our long necks, we can spy a long way off," he said. "We'll find your home for you."

So Pepin, Gilda, and Camelot walked and walked. After a while, they came to a sandy desert.

Camelot lifted his neck and looked all around for a place that was cold and white. Poor Pepin stared down at the sand.

"**Watch out!**" cried Pepin suddenly.

The camel stopped just as his heavy foot was about to crush a small, frightened ant.

"Whew!" sighed the ant. "Thanks for saving my life." Then she stared at Pepin. "What kind of creature are you? I've never seen anyone like you before."

"I'm a penguin," said Pepin. "And I'm lost. My new friends are trying to help me find my way back home."

"I know a path," said the ant. "If you follow it, perhaps it will lead you home."

The three
friends thanked
the ant and followed
her path. Soon, they had left
the sandy desert behind them.

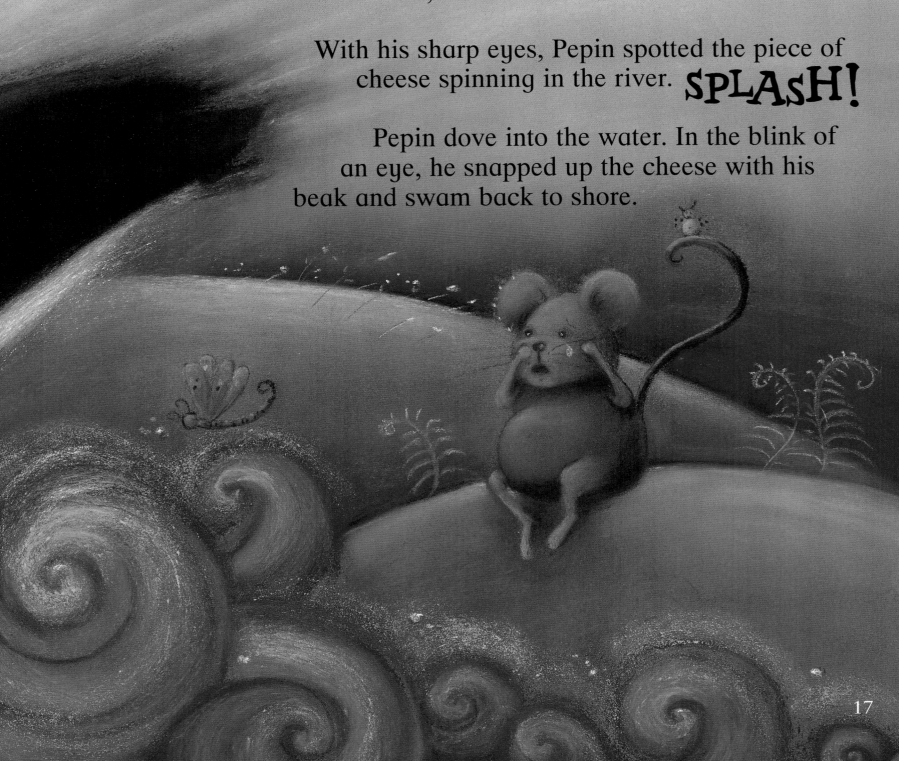

After a while, they came to a raging river.

A small mouse was crying on the riverbank. "I've lost my cheese in the river," he wailed.

With his sharp eyes, Pepin spotted the piece of cheese spinning in the river. SPLASH!

Pepin dove into the water. In the blink of an eye, he snapped up the cheese with his beak and swam back to shore.

17

The mouse was overjoyed.
He broke his cheese into
four pieces and shared it with
his new friends.

"Thanks for saving my dinner," said
the mouse when he had finished
eating. Then he stared at Pepin.
"What kind of creature are you? I've
never seen anyone like you before."

"I'm a penguin," said Pepin. "And I'm lost.
My new friends and I are trying to find the way
back to my home."

The mouse smoothed his whiskers. "I know a path," he squeaked. "If you follow it, perhaps it will lead you home."

19

The three friends thanked the mouse and followed the path. Soon, they had left the raging river behind them.

After a while, they saw that the path led to the foot of a gigantic mountain. "I see some white at the very top," said Gilda, as she stretched her neck. "Perhaps it's your home."

21

The mountain was tall
and steep. The three friends
began the climb to the top.

"**Brrrr!** The wind is cold
here," said Gilda.

"What is all this white on the ground?"
asked Camelot.

"**This is Snow!**" exclaimed Pepin.
"Exactly like we have at my home!"

23

At the top of the snow-covered peak, the three friends found a smiling snowman. Gilda and Camelot had never seen such a thing in the jungle.

Pepin looked around. The peak was perfectly cold and perfectly white, but it was not home.

"I used to make snowmen with Pistachio and Peanut," he said sadly. "But not as nice as this one."

"Thank you," whispered a strange voice.

"Run for your lives!" cried Camelot.
"It's the North Wind!"

The North Wind turned very blue.
"Everyone runs away from me,"
he sighed.

The wind's cold breath felt good
against Pepin's feathers. "Did you
make the snowman?" asked Pepin.

"Yes," said the wind. "I was
playing up here alone.
Everyone hides from me, so I
decided I would hide, too."

"No one likes me," said the North Wind. "They are afraid of me."

"All the penguins are your friends," said Pepin. "Without your cold breath, our land would become too warm. Without your cool breeze, all the ice would melt. You make my home perfect."

The North Wind swelled with happiness.

"AHHHHHHHH!"

He let out a huge, blue, blustery sigh of joy that carried the friends all the way to Pepin's home.

Pepin ran to meet his pretty wife Penelope and their plump chicks Pistachio and Peanut.

"I'll take you back to your home, too," whispered the wind to Gilda and Camelot.

"Thank you," said Gilda. "But first, let's all build a snowman ... together."

Fun facts about Gilda's friends ...

- All penguins live south of the equator. Many of them live on the icy continent of Antarctica.

- Penguins dive into the ocean when they hunt for food. Squid is the favorite treat of many penguins.

- Penguins cannot fly, but they are excellent swimmers.

- Penguins take care of their eggs by balancing them on their toes. This keeps the eggs from resting on the frozen ground.

- Some penguins live on the southern islands of Australia. These birds live in underground burrows or sometimes under houses.

Go on more adventures with Gilda the Giraffe:

Gilda the Giraffe and Leonardo the Lion Cub
Gilda the Giraffe and Lucky the Leopard
Gilda the Giraffe and Marvin the Marmoset
Gilda the Giraffe and Papaya the Panda
No More Melons for Gilda the Giraffe
No Spots for Gilda the Giraffe!

On the Web

FactHound offers a safe, fun way to find Internet sites related to this book. All of the sites on FactHound have been researched by our staff.

Here's how:

1. Visit www.facthound.com

2. Type in this special code for age-appropriate sites: 1404812962

3. Click on the FETCH IT button.

Your trusty FactHound will fetch the best sites for you!